There's a Dragon
IN YOUR BOOK

Written by TOM FLETCHER

Illustrated by GREG ABBOTT

PUFFIN

For Buzz and Buddy – T.F.

For Susanne – G.A.

PUFFIN BOOKS

UK | USA | Canada | Ireland | Australia | India | New Zealand | South Africa

Puffin Books is part of the Penguin Random House group of companies whose
addresses can be found at global.penguinrandomhouse.com.

www.penguin.co.uk
www.puffin.co.uk
www.ladybird.co.uk

Penguin
Random House
UK

First published 2018

001

Copyright © Tom Fletcher, 2018
Illustrated by Greg Abbott

The moral right of the author has been asserted

Printed in China

A CIP catalogue record for this book is available from the British Library

ISBN: 978–0–141–37612–7

All correspondence to:
Puffin Books, Penguin Random House Children's, 80 Strand, London WC2R 0RL

OH LOOK!

There's an egg in your book!

It looks ready to hatch.
Whatever you do, don't turn the page . . .

I can't believe you did that!

The egg has hatched and now there's a
dragon in your book!

Don't be scared – it's a baby dragon!

Why don't you **tickle** her little nose . . .

ACHOO!

Oops!

The dragon accidentally sneezed
a fire in your book.

We need to
put it out quickly.

Help Dragon **blow** out the flame
and turn the page.

OH NO!

Your dragon didn't blow the fire out –
she blew MORE fire!

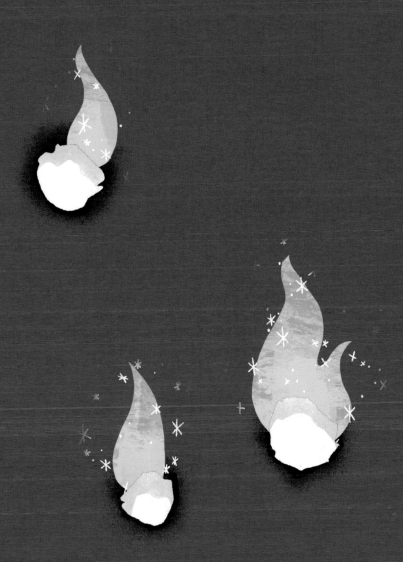

Carefully cover the flames
by turning the page –
that should put them out!

That's no good . . .
the fire is getting bigger!

Don't get
too close!

If only we could think of a way
to put out this fire . . .

THAT'S IT!

Let's use your *imagination*

to put the fire out!

IMAGINE

a great big water balloon
right in the middle of the next page.

Make sure it's full and ready to pop . . .

PERFECT!

Now use your finger to **PoP** the balloon and get ready for the . . .

Hooray! You put the fire out.

Give the dragon a
HIGH FIVE!

You have a great imagination – and Dragon
must be a little hungry now . . .

Why don't you use your imagination again
and think up a **yummy treat** for her?

How about a great big cone filled with
a triple scoop of scrummy,

yummy,

ice-cold,

chocolate-and-strawberry-flavoured . . .

Ice cream!

(With sprinkles.)

Wow! That looks delicious.

Yum!

Well, Dragon must be tired
after all that adventure.
I think it's time for her to fly home.

She looks very full – she's going to
need some help taking off.

Flap the book up and down like giant dragon wings . . .

Nearly there –
keep flapping!

There she goes!

Goodbye, Dragon!

Wave goodbye and turn the . . .

Hang on a second . . .
What's this?

Oh look –
more eggs!